MAGIC & MEMORIES

By
Ann Parker

Illustrated by Harvey Padmore

ShieldCrest

ISBN: 978-1-913839-80-2

MMXXI

A CIP catalogue record for this is available from the
British Library

Published by
ShieldCrest Publishing,
Bicker, Lincs, PE20 3BT England
Tel: +44 (0) 333 8000 890
www.shieldcrest.co.uk

Dedicated with love to Terry, Emma & Louise and to all my family for always loving me, so I knew just what to write in these stories.

And a special thanks to Jim & Lillian Fidler in Canada and my friend, Jane, for their encouragement and listening to my poems.

Not forgetting my heartfelt gratitude to Harvey for his wonderful illustrations.

Contents

Introduction

Ages 5 - 11

This illustrated children's book contains 20 rhyming verse, short stories. They are the perfect length for bedtime stories and easy to read when the child can read for themselves.

There are fantasy and mystery tales like Erik the Elf, Mermaids & Miracles and a superhero unicorn, as well as heart-warming family stories of Grandpas and Nannies.

Funny ones, spooky ones, even a football one. In Roary the Cat adults will find hidden references like 'Milk is a dish best served cold' and lots of funny puns. All stories feature friendship, kindness and belonging.

As an added bonus it features the full-length story of Lady Isadora, the wickedly good 'Witch of Ridgebone Manor', the first in a series of books.

It's the perfect gift, where you can write on the first page 'with love from...' and your child or grandchild will want to cherish it forever.

The Bravest Badger

A stranger strolled into Apple Tree Farm.

Sheepdog jumped up to sound the alarm.

"You can't come in here, it's farm animals only."

"Well, would you believe I'm a very small pony?"

"No. You don't belong here," Sheepdog said in disgust.

"I've no idea what you are, but you're not one of us."

"I'm Badger," he said. "And I've come a long way."

"I'd be ever so grateful if you let me stay."

"We'll have to discuss it," said Horse to the dog.

"But what good would you be? We all have jobs."

"Just moooove out the way," said a black and white cow.

"Can you supply milk? I don't think so somehow."

The chickens came over, with their beaks in the air.

"We lay the eggs. What have you got to share?"

Badger said "I can dig very big holes."

"I see," said Cow, rudely. "You're just a big mole."

Horse said, "I carry men on my back."

"But your legs are short, so you couldn't do that."

Turkey went over and stretched out her wings.

"I'm a VIP guest, amongst other things"

"I've invites for Christmas and maybe Thanksgiving."

"There's nothing your kind can do for a living."

Pig said, "I'm known for my very fine ham."

"Don't know what it is, but I do what I can."

"And for Christmas, I hear, I'm getting a blanket."

"Even talk of me going to a very posh banquet."

"Our wool is the softest around," said the sheep.

"If you could do something, you might earn your keep."

4

"I can't lay an egg, not that I've tried."

"And I've only my friendship to give," he replied.

"But I've travelled so far, could I stay for a sleep?"

Sheepdog said, "Just for one night, with the sheep."

Badger felt an outsider and just in the way.

But despite feeling lonesome, he slept in the hay.

It was dark when he woke and he heard a strange sound.

He sniffed the cold air and sensed danger around.

He crept from the barn while the others all slept.

When he saw four red eyes, he fearlessly leapt.

He shouted out "FOX" and he woke up the farm.

And raced to the chickens to save them from harm.

The foxes ran out of the henhouse in fright.

Badger chased them away to the black of the night.

The chickens were crying and shaking in shock.

"You saved our lives, Badger. We owe you a lot."

"How did you know there was trouble?" asked Pig.

"I'm beginning to think you can do more than just dig."

"I'm nocturnal," said Badger. "I don't sleep at night."

"I can't stay up in the daytime, try as I might."

"Would you be willing," asked Pig, Cow and Horse,

"To stay here and guard us? We'll pay you of course."

"There's no need for that, just my food and a bed."

"I'm sorry we weren't very nice," Sheepdog said.

"But we've all learned a lesson and know we were wrong."

"We shouldn't have said you didn't belong."

The chickens and turkeys all begged him to stay.

And a badger became a farm animal that day.

The foxes vanished from sight and did no more harm.

And now strangers are welcomed at Apple Tree Farm.

Just don't come at night and break in the yard.

There's a brave little badger, who's their security guard.

The Thimble and the Leprechaun

I went to Auntie's because Mum was sick.

I actually think that she is a witch.

She lives in a cottage that's full to the brim,

With a cat that hisses when you look at him.

And there's hundreds of thimbles up on a shelf.

Then she had to go out and leave me by myself.

"Look at my collection, but whatever you do,"

"Don't put on the thimble that's yellow and blue."

Well I tried not to look at the item in question

And started off with the best of intentions.

9

But hey, I'm a kid, it looked like the rest.

So it went on my finger to do a test.

At first nothing happened, I needn't have feared.

But to my surprise a leprechaun appeared.

"Thank you," he said. "You have lifted my curse."

Uh-oh I thought, this day just got worse.

The leprechaun laughed now the curse had gone

And said it was his fault as he had done wrong.

"The Fairytale Queen put this curse on me."

"When you hear what I did, I'm sure you'll agree."

"It was me that pushed Humpty off that wall."

"And Jack and Jill didn't just fall."

"And you've heard the story of three little kittens,"

"Who do you think kept hiding their mittens?"

He went on to say why the weasel went pop

And why all of a sudden that bough had just dropped.

And believe it or not, you know Bo Peep?

Turns out it wasn't her fault that she lost her sheep.

The leprechaun grinned as he made his escape.

Sometimes I wonder how I get in these scrapes.

Should I tell my aunt? Not on your nelly.

I put back the thimble and turned on the telly.

But over the weeks I heard a few things,

Like there's no wings for angels, when a bell rings.

And the Easter Bunny has lost her eggs

And all five monkeys were pushed off the bed.

Not only that, a little Miss Muffet

Had a big black spider put on her tuffet.

But my leprechaun helped me, once or twice.
Took me off the naughty list onto the nice.
And the tooth fairy came the other night
With double the cash when it wasn't that white.
Will that naughty leprechaun ever be found
Before London Bridge starts falling down?

Now would you believe I'm at Auntie's again?

Things were all going fine for a while, but then...

"Oh, by the way, whatever you do,"

"Don't pick up the gold horseshoe."

So I tried not to look at the item in question

And started off with the best of intentions.

But hey, I'm a kid, you can't blame me.

Maybe I'll just go and see...

14

Letter To Grandpa

Dear Grandpa, it's Freddie. I hope you are well.

Please give my love to Nana as well.

It's been a few months, so I thought I had better,

Tell you I miss you and write you a letter.

I was thinking of times we had gone to the park.

And you taught me to tell trees and flowers apart.

The pinecones we found are still next to my bed.

When Dad trod on one, can't repeat what he said.

All that I know is when I said it once,

I was threatened that I would be grounded for months.

You were often in trouble with Mummy as well.

Like Auntie Jane's wedding, you got tipsy and fell.

Once we drove on the driveway and you let me steer

And she saw when you gave me a sip of your beer.

I wonder if Dad knew you always brought sweets

Or when I'd been naughty you'd sneak me in treats.

I've a confession myself, remember your mat?

It was me knocked your cup off, it wasn't the cat.

And that time that your cuckoo clock suddenly stopped.

It hadn't just broke, it was 'cos it was dropped.

But I'd never worry that you'd shout at me.

I'd always get round you and sit on your knee.

Telling me stories while here babysitting,

Of how you met Nana and she'd be sat knitting.

How you'd given up girlfriends as she was the one.

And started a family and that was my mum.

You don't babysit now and that I regret.

I know I am older, but don't love you less.

Just to go fishing, I'd give anything.

With our nets and our sun hats and jam jars on string.

Holidays with you were always great fun.

We camped in the rain and sailed in the sun.

But you've not been so active over the years.

And when Mum and Dad talk I often see tears.

Dad said you've gone to a much better place.

Can't you come to visit? I so miss your face.

I thought that I'd seen you a couple of times.

But it was someother Grandpa. It wasn't mine.

Let's make a plan to go and play ball

And blow some more bubbles, like when I was small.

Then fish on the lake, but we'll take it slow.

You don't have to worry, 'cos now I can row.

Please let me know when you're able to come.

And thank you again for all you have done.

But wait just a minute, Mum's told me the news.

Can't believe you and Nana are coming here soon.

Nobody told me, it's all been discussed,

You hated that home and will move in with us.

So now I can read to you, like you did me.

Or push you round the park and look at the trees.

I'm so happy, Grandad, that I got my wish

To see you and Nana. Love Freddie. Kiss Kiss.

19

20

Roary & the Feral Feline Felony

Newfoundland is known more for its dogs than its cats.

But there's a little, grey tabby about to change that.

One day he'll feature in poems and songs.

His name's Roary and he was born in St. John's.

He was sad as a kitten, because he was teased

For not wanting to hurt a bird or a bee.

As luck had it, he moved to the perfect home.

The service was good, he rarely needed to moan.

So, with Lillian and Jim, he decided to stay

And had them both trained in a matter of days.

Roary was pleased with a staff of two.

Very handy for when he got stuck on the roof.

Jim told Roary, "Don't go too far."

And for the first few days, he stayed in the yard.

Till he met Tallulah, the white cat next door

And together they went to prowl and explore.

Those hot summer days, they walked in the hills

And stayed out till dawn, then it started to chill.

As the nights grew long and the leaves turned brown,

The Cataloni brothers moved into town.

One was big and mean and a ginger tom

With a scar on his face and his name was Don.

He wore a thick collar, covered in spikes

And his eyes were green but shone red at night.

The other was Bugsy, not quite so hard.

But he did what Don said, as he was in charge.

Within a month, they both owned the streets.

It was fated that he and Roary would meet.

Don sat on the sidewalk, inspecting his claws.

A mouse was held by its tail, under his paw.

Roary arched up his back and approached really slow.

"That's my friend Molly. Please let her go."

"We meet at last, Roary," and he let go the mouse.

And leapt at our hero and chased him to his house.

He got home and jumped on the roof to escape.

Thankful that Molly the mouse was now safe.

By winter, the brothers were running the night.

Nobody dared to put up a fight.

Catnapping, milk theft and gambling dens,

And bootlicking gangs were all run by them.

Loan sharks lent you a fish, but you gave them back
two,

Or they'd make you an offer, you couldn't refuse.

The Valentine's Day mouseacre was the final straw.

The mice weren't allowed in the town anymore.

Roary heard of a cat, Ness was his name,

And cleaning up crime was his claim to fame.

He told Roary the story of Al Catone.

The meanest cat that ever did roam.

Who ran the city with an iron paw.

Mouse-catching rings, furball fights, snuggling and more.

"If you didn't obey," Ness had said,

"You'd wake up with something bad in your bed."

"You know that milk is a dish best served cold."

And told him to listen to what he was told.

He explained how Catone had at last been caught.

"I'll have to catch Don the same way," Roary thought.

He left with a plan, knowing just what to do.

And told Tallulah and friends, so they could help too.

"Tonight Bugsy and Don are locked up for good."

"It's time to take back our neighbourhood."

"We need a box and a net and a length of twine."

"Plus old Mrs Cook, at house number nine."

They crept up on Bugsy, holding the box,

Put it over his head and sat on the top.

For Roary, it was a much more risky assail,

He let out a roar and grabbed Don by his tail.

Don whipped round his head, while baring his teeth.

The green eyes flashed red and he started to hiss.

Roary took off, as fast as he could,

Down the alleys, to house number nine by the wood.

27

He leapt in the backyard and picked up the net.

But Don was too strong and he got it instead.

"Any last wishes?" asked the fearsome crook.

Then they heard a loud rumble and both stopped to look.

All they could see was hundreds of mice.

Led by Molly, who Roary had once saved her life.

They wrapped Don in the net and tied it up tight.

Roary pulled off his collar, avoiding the bites.

The plan had gone well just one part left now.

Roary went to the door and began to meow.

Mrs Cook came out and said, "What's going on?"

"Oh, you're trapped little kitty" and she picked up Don.

"You've not got a collar, you must be a stray."

"I'll keep you safely inside, then you can't get away."

That's how Roary had saved their neighbourhood

And Don Cataloni was locked up for good.

Bugsy gave in as he'd lost all his powers

And they all celebrated till the early hours.

Roary got home and stretched out on the bed.

"Cats have such an easy life," Lillian said.

"It must be quite boring, as well," said Jim.

"We'll treat him and let him play with some string."

Roary rolled his eyes and began to think,

It's amazing that humans are not yet extinct.

As for Don, he turned into the perfect house cat.

He's looked after well and is getting quite fat.

Turns out he preferred the life he now had.

It was much easier to be good than bad.

So Tallulah and Roary can now walk around

The hills and the streets of their hometown.

The Magical Dressmaker's Shop

I grew up in Ireland. Just me and my mum.

We were poorer than most, but richer than some.

When I was young I was told of a shop.

It had a red and white door with a bell on the top.

Mum told me about the dressmaker there,

Who made clothes for the fairies and pixies to wear.

The shopkeeper seemed to know just what you'd need.

And never took payment, just pass on a good deed.

She made me my party dress when I was six.

Mum said there was magic in every stitch.

It was a light shade of blue and covered in lace.

And a skirt that twirled out and a sash round my
waist.

For my first day at school, the shop sent me a bag.

Not leather, like most, but I wasn't sad.

Mine had good luck sewn in all of the seams.

Held not only my books, but also my dreams.

My warm, winter coat was also bewitching.

There were wishes and fortune in all of the stitching.

The buttons were made of mother of pearl.

Crafted by fairies for good little girls.

Mum went many times, when I was small

To get magical presents. I remember them all.

I never thought of the shop after I'd grown.

And when mum passed away, I went back to my home.

I was cold in the house with no fire in the hearth

Then remembered her smile and the sound of her laugh.

I went up to the attic, where I'd never been

And started to cry at what I had seen.

A sewing machine, next to a very old light.

Had my poor mum been working all hours of the night?

In a chest on the floor was a big pile of rags.

And the one on the top was the same as my bag.

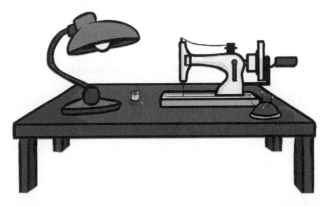

Bits of a man's shirt matched my dress shade of blue.

And an old net curtain had been cut in two.

The sleeves made a sash and a cuff made the bow.

She made sure I felt beautiful and would never know.

I'd gone to my party and felt like a queen.

Friends said it was the nicest that they'd ever seen.

My coat, I could see, had been cut from a quilt.

And I found an old blanket the same as my kilt.

With all of the scraps was a memory for each.

Like Christmas and birthdays, or walks on the beach.

My mum was the one who had sewn every stitch.

So I never felt poor and always felt rich.

Under the rags, in an old shoe box,

I found Annie, the ragdoll I got from the shop.

She always to me was my luckiest charm.

But it hadn't been magic that kept me from harm.

My mum kept me safe, throughout all of those years.

"I love you, Mummy," I said through the tears.

I left our old house and looked up at the sign.

FOR SALE it said, but it had to be mine.

So now Annie, the ragdoll sleeps on my bed.

She looked after me, now it's my turn instead.

I think of Mummy in Heaven, in a dressmaker's shop.
With a red and white door and a bell on the top,
Making dresses for angels and mending their wings
And for all of the children, making wonderful things.

"Slow down, Alfie Brown"

When Alfie was born, it was said he came early.

And was ever so cute, with black hair that was curly.

He was still very small when he started to crawl

On his hands and his knees at super fast speed.

At nine months he walked and the trouble begun

'Cos it didn't stop there, as now he could run.

"Slow down, Alfie Brown," but he never did.

Or wouldn't sit still like all other kids.

As for poor Grandma, when she'd babysit,

She felt totally shattered and very unfit.

His first day at school, the teachers could see

He ran, talked and ate as fast as could be.

"Have you ants in your pants?" one asked Alfie
Brown.

So he felt very sad when he had to sit down.

Out in the playground the children played IT

But they never caught him 'cos he was too quick.

At the age of eleven, he started big school.

"No running inside," now was the rule.

40

But someone said he shouldn't slow down.

He had a plan for the fast Alfie Brown.

A football coach watched a match in the park

When Alfie and friends were all taking part.

Where he ran past his mates and scored all the goals.

"No one can mark him," the person was told.

Alfie was the best player he'd ever seen.

So asked him to play for his famous team.

Alfie signed with his club and was soon well known,

Winning twenty one cups by the time he had grown.

Till one day he stood at a World Cup match.

Captain's band on, number ten on his back.

Alfie looked at his family and gave them a wave

As his dad thought back to his childhood days.

How their little boy had never slowed down

And the chants from the crowd were for his Alfie
Brown.

At the sound of the whistle, he took the first kick

And ran up the pitch, he really was quick.

He tried a long shot and it went in the net.

One nil to the hosts, but was not over yet.

Before extra time it was two goals all.

Then Alfie ran fast and got hold of the ball.

He went round one player, then past the next,

Into his half, just the goalie was left.

With ten seconds to go he kicked the ball.

But time stood still till he heard the roar.

They'd won the World Cup thanks to Alfie Brown.

And from that day on his life never slowed down.

Erik the Elf

There's a time and place between night and day,
When you can visit a land where unicorns play.
And fairies and giants live side by side.
Where mermaids swim and dragons fly.

But the King of the trolls had a terrible plight.
He just couldn't get to sleep at night.
One day he made a proclamation.
And put up a reward to all the nation.
"A pot of gold is yours to keep"
"If anyone can make me sleep."
Well news of this spread through the land.
And many went to try their hand.

A fairy was the first to try
With some sleeping dust above his eyes.
But the King of the trolls was not pleased,
As all it did was make him sneeze.

A witch came next with a slimy brew.
Frogs and bats all stirred in a stew.
"A cup at night is the perfect dose."
But still the King just was not close.

A giant rocked him back and forth.
The King felt sick and made it worse.
Neither wizards, pixies or magic rings,
Nor a pillow made of angel's wings
Could make the King nod off and dream.
"He's awfully grumpy," said the Queen.

But meanwhile in the palace kitchen,

An elf called Erik started thinking.

Since he was three, he'd had a power,

He couldn't stop, he'd talk for hours.

If he told a tale he thought it odd

That eyes would close and heads would nod.

And just don't ask if he's okay,

You'll never get to walk away.

His family got earplugs and nodded and smiled,

And said "Yes, dear. No, dear," once in a while.

He'd give his thoughts but that poor elf,

Would end up talking to himself.

Erik thought of the King and the big pot of gold,

"You could send off a saint," he'd always been told.

That night he crept up and knocked on his door.

"Who's there?" said the King with an ominous roar.

"Excuse me, your highness, my voice has a gift."

"You'll sleep like a baby, asleep in its crib."

"I've no faith in elves," the King replied.

"But I've nothing to lose, so you might as well try."

The King put on his nightcap and lay on his bed.

Erik sat on a chair. "Here's my story," he said.

He started his tale from when he was two,

How he'd always loved cabbage and things that were blue.

Well just when the King couldn't stand anymore,

An amazing thing happened - he started to snore.

He slept for five hours, as Erik got to age ten,

So it wasn't surprising, the King slept again.

After one week of Erik, he slept like a rock.

Sometimes he'd pretend 'cos that elf never stopped.

Like, did he know there's an insect that looks like a stick?

And the oldest elf was two hundred and six?

Just the thought of that voice sent him out like a light.

So he gave him the gold and made him a knight.

Erik had the last laugh, like he never dreamt.

He had waves and cheers wherever he went.

His fans arrived from all over the kingdom,

Hoping to hear Erik's stories and wisdom.

Now he lives in a castle with family I'm told,

And shares not just his thoughts, but also his gold.

His bedtime story is a bestselling book.

And if your children won't sleep, please take a look.

Read it at night, it'll send them away

To where fairies and pixies and unicorns play.

Bella's Christmas Wish

"Wake up, Bella. We've got a surprise."

With a smile and a giggle she opened her eyes.

"It's the day before Christmas, so Lily and you,"

"Need to jump out of bed 'cos we're off to the zoo."

After having their breakfast and loading the car,

They started the journey. It wasn't that far.

A very posh tiger said "How do you do?"

"I say, would you let me spend Christmas with you?"

"I don't think that you should," Bella said, sweetly.

"I'm sure you are nice, but I'm worried you'd eat me."

"Is it chilly up there?" Bella asked a giraffe.

"With the length of my neck, I could do with a scarf."

"My nanny could knit one in yellow and red."

"I wouldn't need that if I slept on your bed."

"I wish that you could, but being so tall,"

"I very much doubt you could get in the hall."

"Good day," said a monkey and joined in their picnic,

Stealing the cake and eating the biscuits."

"I know this is cheeky, but that's what I do,"

"I just wondered if I could have Christmas with you?"

"I'm not being funny, but you are a bit playful."

"You'd gobble the food and leave none on the table."

A big crocodile came along for a chat.

"Can I come with you? I'm not going to snap."

"I'm glad that you're friendly and up for a laugh,"

"But sorry," said Bella. "You won't fit in my bath."

A slippery snake slithered over to say,

"Surely you've got room for me Christmas day?"

"I'm sorry to say I've got other plans."

"But if I'm being honest, I'm afraid of your fangs."

"Just one sleep till Christmas," said a cuddly brown bear.

"But please take me with you. It is only fair."

"I wish that I could," as she tickled his belly."

"Though I don't think I can, as you're awfully smelly."

Bella felt very sad as she waved them goodbye.

She felt a bit guilty and thought she might cry.

It was getting quite dark when she got in the car.

"I wish I could keep them," she said to a star.

54

That night before Christmas, she lay in her bed

And heard a kerfuffle. "Who's there?" Bella said.

There was a strange sound and it gave her a fright.

So she sat up in bed and turned on the light.

A giraffe, snake and tiger were snuggling there.

And a cheeky monkey sat on a chair.

A crocodile lay on the end of her bed.

"We've turned into toys," he happily said.

"You wished on the Christmas star," said the bear.

"So we're here to protect you. We'll always be there."

Bella got them in bed and gave them all kisses.

"I'm so happy you're here and we all got our wishes."

Together they listened for Santa above,

But they needed no presents as now they had love.

George's Racetrack Race

It was one of those Sundays when the rain was
falling.

In George's opinion it was all very boring.

"I'm bored, Dad. Can you play with me?"

"Come and sit here and watch the Grand Prix."

"That's boring, Dad." So he went to his room.

But he'd got an idea for that wet afternoon.

"I'll get out my racetrack, it can't be that hard."

He joined it together and put on the cars.

There was a bright yellow one, but he preferred red.

"It's time for the race," a tiny voice said.

A little man stood right next to the track.

"I'm your mechanic and my name is Jack."

Suddenly the cars began to get big.

"No, I'm getting smaller," George started to think.

Soon he became the same size as the man.

"What on earth's happened? I don't understand."

"You've got to race the champion, called Mark."

"You'll have to hurry. It's about to start."

George then noticed the crowds in the stands.

People were cheering and clapping their hands.

He got in the red car and sat in the seat,

"But, Jack, I can't drive, I'm bound to get beat."

"Of course you know just what to do."

"You've been playing with cars since you were two."

The countdown started then away they went.

George gripped the wheel till it almost bent.

Yellow pulled off and left Red on the grid.

George put his foot down and went off with a skid.

With a squeal of tyres and smoke from the rubber,

Red roared off to catch up with the other.

Mark had a four second lead by then.

George went too fast and came off at the bend.

He steered to the left and got back on line.

But that made him even further behind.

He caught up a bit, Mark was slightly ahead.

"You can do this, George," said a voice in his head.

Just one more lap, it was now or never.

As the red car got close, Mark made an error.

He over steered and was going so fast

George changed gear and went flying past.

So the red car took the chequered flag.

The crowd got to its feet, they really were glad.

George slowed down for a victory lap.

Even Mark was impressed and started to clap.

On the podium he got a champion's cup.

He gave it a kiss and held it up.

As he looked at the trophy he began to think

Am I getting bigger or is it starting to shrink?

He grew and grew till he got to his height

As his mum walked in to check he was alright.

"You missed the Grand Prix. It was a great race."

"No I didn't," said George. "I got first place."

"I see," said Mum. "You've been playing cars too."

"I don't remember that cup. Did Dad buy it for you?"

"I'm trying to tell you I won in the red."

Mum just smiled at George and patted his head.

He made the decision the next time it rained

He'd get out his railway and drive his own train.

Supercorn & the Dragon

Tilly the unicorn sat on her own.

Unlike her friends, she hadn't grown.

At school the others all called her Titch.

To be big like them was her only wish.

Playtime they made her piggy in the middle

And some of them even sang a riddle.

"Who's the smallest unicorn?"

"With the little baby horn."

"Who's the one that's very silly?"

"It's teeny weeny, tiny Tilly."

She'd never cry but stood up tall

Knowing one day she would show them all

On sportsday morning, Tilly got out of bed,

"Mummy, I'm not going to school" she said.

"They always tease me because I come last."

"So please can I stay at home?" she asked.

But Grandma said "I've an itchy horn."

"It won't take place, there'll be a frightful storm."

"Thunder and lightning will soon be coming."

"Don't worry, Tilly, you won't be running."

But the egg and horn race did go ahead.

And in the six legged one she fell on her head.

Then it was time to jump in a sack.

Tilly got in and stood on the track.

But one of the boys tied up the top,

Teasing and laughing as they ran off.

But the giggles turned to screams of fear.

She couldn't see and could only hear,

As the teachers and unicorns fled to the school

Leaving Tilly scared and trembling too.

She was able to get her head out the sack,

As the sun went in and the clouds turned black.

Only then could Tilly see,

Why all the others had to flee.

A dragon was breathing fire and smoke.

Standing up to him was their only hope.

The sack caught on her mane as she made her escape

And Tilly thought it looked like a cape.

It made her think of Superman,

And with Grandma's words she thought of a plan,

That the dragon would think she had superpowers

To make the sky flash and the winds to howl.

"Dragon," she shouted. "I'm Supercorn."

"If you hurt my friends, you'll feel my scorn."

The dragon said "You may try."

"But one breath from me and your cape will fry."

"Well," said Tilly, "You may huff and puff,"

"But I am made of superstuff."

"If you're so fierce and I'm so small,"

"Let's see who's the greatest one of all."

Dragon looked at a bush and breathed over it,

Till all that was left was some blackened twigs.

"That's nothing," said Tilly. "The skies will light,"

"Then I'll shake the earth with all my might."

Suddenly they heard a clap of thunder.

The dragon shook with awe and wonder

As a tree was hit by a bolt of lightning.

Even to Tilly, it was very frightening.

The sky lit up in a blaze of light.

Grandma's itchy horn was right.

The dragon bowed down and sank to his knees.

"Supercorn, don't hurt me please."

Tilly promised she wouldn't and in the end

They finished up forever friends.

The others crept out and apologised,

'Cos they'd been mean and she'd saved their lives.

And the whole school of unicorns,

Did a guard of honour with their horns.

They knew that they had all been wrong,

So now they sang a different song.

"Who's the bravest unicorn?"

"With the little baby horn."

"Who can take on any quest?"

"Supercorn, 'cos she's the best."

She won the Sportsday Cup that day,

For scaring that naughty dragon away.

Tilly may have been small with a baby horn,

But they all looked up to Supercorn.

She grew and grew till the age of ten,

Would you believe she was bigger than them?

She still puts on her cape from time to time,

If the goblins or monsters get out of line.

And went on to be the best loved unicorn,

Thanks to Mother Nature and Grandma's horn.

The Mystery Of The Ragdoll

I found an old ragdoll by my front door.

My mum said she'd never seen it before.

It looked rather unloved sat all on its own.

So I asked Mum if we could give her a home.

"It smells and it's filthy," my mother replied.

But I didn't care, I took her inside.

Mum wasn't wrong, she really did stink.

But looked better after a bath in the sink.

71

I couldn't help wonder to whom she belonged

And was that person sad, that now she had gone?

She had buttons for eyes and a worn out face

And a tatty old dress, that was edged with white lace.

The wool for her hair was tangled and thin.

At that moment my horrible brother burst in.

"What a spooky old thing, it's as ugly as sin."

"It gives me the creeps. It should go in the bin."

Just like magic, a book hit him square on his head.

"Who threw that?" said my terrified brother and
fled.

Well, I may be wrong, but I know what I saw,

My doll gave me a smile as he ran out the door.

I said "Don't worry, Katy, of course you can stay."

Her name appeared in my mind in a very strange
way.

I had no way of knowing if this was her name,

But I just had a feeling I couldn't explain.

73

That night Katy sat on the end of my bed,

When I woke she was snuggled right next to my head.

For some reason I knew, I shouldn't be scared,

She just needed a friend, to show someone cared.

One day, I took her to school in my bag.

My friends might have made fun of my doll made of rags.

As I made my way home, I heard someone shout "STOP."

And just missed a car that pulled out by a shop.

There was no one about but Katy and me.

Had she just saved my life? It looked like it to me.

From that day on, she stayed by my side.

And it's funny, I thought, did she always have eyes?

Weren't they black buttons? I could be wrong.

And since when was her hair so silky and long?

Her clothes were now made from the finest of
cotton.

New life for a toy that was long ago forgotten.

Her face looked so much more happy too.

Perhaps to be loved, her real beauty shone through.

We had many adventures over the years.

Then something happened that was really quite weird.

We found black and white photos, in an old tin.

It had uncles and aunties and great grandparents in.

Then I found one that gave me a shock,

Of a girl and her doll in an old-fashioned frock.

On the back it was dated as eighteen hundred and eighty.

And it was great great Aunt Mabel and her new doll, called Katy.

Well Mabel and me, we looked just the same.

I was no longer surprised that I knew Katy's name.

Where she'd been all those years, would never be
known.

But somehow she'd managed to find her way home.

Now we have a daughter, who we named Mabel

Watched over by Katy, as she sleeps in her cradle.

Rascal's River Rescue

At their grandfather's house on the River Thames,

Layla and Max spent the summer weekends.

His boat was named Rascal and made of wood

With gaff rigged sails and a canvas hood.

It had no engine so it needed the wind.

And the tide helped as well going out and in.

Grandfather let them sail on their own

With life jackets on and to stay close to home.

This one day they moored under a willow tree

And had cake and sandwiches for their tea.

A swan and her cygnets swam alongside,

So they threw bits of bread as they bobbed and dived.

An elderly couple started shouting and waved,

"Our engine is broken, we're floating away."

"The tide has caught us and soon we could be"

"Dragged by the current and out to sea."

Layla and Max quickly pulled up the sails

And just managed to hook the other boat's rails.

With a rope on their boat they towed them to shore.

The elderly pair couldn't thank them more.

"Without your help, what would we have done?"

"Things aren't so easy when you're not young."

But one week later, the young ones were in need.

Rascal was stuck in the mud and the reeds.

They were getting scared as the tide rushed in

'Cos they couldn't move, as there was no wind.

But then just when they had given up hope

The old couple came and threw them a rope.

"A good turn deserves another," they said.

And they towed Layla and Max, in Rascal instead.

They all went back to Grandfather's place,

Where they moored the boats safely and had tea and cakes.

The Timekeeper's Wizard

It was Luke's birthday party when this story took place.

There was his little brother and six of his mates.

Then just as the clock had chimed half past four,

There was a big gust of wind and a knock at the door.

A red-haired magician was standing outside.

He had a black and gold bag with a star on the side.

"Come through to the garden. They're playing out there."

Luke's mum left him to it and flopped on a chair.

He bowed to the children and sat them in a line.

"I'm the Timekeeper's Wizard and can travel in time."

"Luke, it's your choice, when would you like to visit?"

"Well I like dinosaurs, so I think the Jurassic"

"You should know," said the man, "That wherever we
go,"

"No one can see us, our hosts never know."

He took out of his bag a digital clock.

He punched in some numbers and then they were off.

They were shocked at the size of the huge dinosaurs,

And the size of their feet and their razor-sharp
claws.

Zak tried to warn Alex but he didn't see,

A big pile of poo that came up to his knees.

Lewis was the brainy one of their year,

"Please could I go and see William Shakespeare?"

So they went to the Globe and watched a new play,

Called Romeo and Doreen, as it was on that day.

Reece fancied a look at Victorian times.

But didn't expect the fog and the grime.

People looked poor and the children all worked.

"We have it easy," the time travellers thought.

Jacob chose pirates aboard a big ship,

But that ended quick when the waves made him sick.

"I know," said Harvey. "Can we go forward in time?"

"Yes," said the wizard. "That will be fine."

The timepiece was set for eighty years time.

They'd be a lot older, about eighty nine.

The houses were square and all made of wood

And on each flat roof, a flying car stood.

There were trees and lakes and grass, nicely mowed.

No need for concrete, there weren't any roads.

The sky was clear and a bright shade of blue.

The sun powered the earth and at night the moon too.

Back at the house Mum and Dad had a fright,

"Where on earth have they gone? Luke is grounded for life."

Just as they called the police on the phone,

They heard laughter and chatter. "Thank goodness, they're home."

The mothers and fathers to collect, came around

Wondered why Alex smelled and his legs were all brown.

"Such imaginations," one father said.

"Pirates, flying cars and a tyrannosaurus rex."

"It's the truth," said Jacob. "We jumped millions of years."

But the one that could prove it had just disappeared.

"Where did you book him?" Mum said to Dad.

"I didn't book him. I thought that you had."

They never did find out how he came to be

At Luke's birthday party. It's a real mystery.

So please take a minute to think where you'd see.

There's so much to choose from in earth's history.

"If you choose prehistoric," young Alex said,

"Wear very long boots and watch where you tread."

Liliana's First Winter

There's something white falling. Mum says it's snow.

Who's making that mess I'd like to know.

Perhaps it's the snowman Mum's talking about.

I just hope he can't get in the house.

And one other thing, a tree has appeared.

It's covered in balls. That really is weird.

Now there's two stockings up on the shelf.

And don't get me started on that naughty elf.

There's lights everywhere and holly galore.

What on earth's happening, I can't take anymore.

Lanterns and cards are strung up on string.

My sister knows why but she won't say a thing.

Mum keeps singing 'bout a jingling bell.

Daddy's gone shopping. Why can't I go as well?

Today I was put in a funny red hat.

A man's come down the chimney. How scary is that?

But hang on a minute, this stocking's for me.

It says it's from Santa, whoever he'd be.

It's full up with toys all covered in wrapping.

Mum can forget it, there's no way I'm napping.

Then we had a big meal with something called
sprouts.

Just so you know – I spat them all out.

The others pulled something that made a loud bang.

Give babies a heads up next time if you can.

I got so many toys, they were in a huge mound,

And the next day Nanny and Grandad came round.

What more presents? I could get used to this.

"Merry Christmas," says Nan. So that's what this is.

Things went back to normal, then would you believe

There's a special night called New Year's Eve?

There's not any presents, just fireworks and fun

And lots of wishes and kisses from everyone.

Winter was my new, best time of the year

Till I heard there's a bunny who brings chocolate eggs here.

And then there's birthdays, with candles and cake.

And even more presents. I really can't wait.

It's a wonderful life, of that there's no doubt,

Just promise we'll never have any more sprouts!!

Holly's Halloween Horror

My name is Holly and I've a story to share.

It was last October but still gives me nightmares.

A castle near us had a Halloween Tour.

I went with my family and we paid at the door.

A witch with a large black wart took the money.

You could see it was stuck on, I'm not being funny.

Skeletons to the left and bats to the right.

All made out of plastic, but still gave me a fright.

In one of the rooms was an old rocking chair.

"Hello, little girl," said the man that sat there.

"My name is Lord Ken. Can I be your guide?"

"I've lived here for years." "Of course," I replied.

His clothes were the oldest that I've ever seen.

We went to a dungeon, where I let out a scream.

Chained to the wall was a man who looked scary.

I don't want to be rude but he really was hairy.

"It's a full moon tonight," he said with a growl.

"Perfect for werewolves," and let out a howl.

Ken pulled me out quickly and said "Let's find my parents."

"They're vampires and love to eat, I mean meet with the peasants."

Beside a large fireplace the two of them sat.

They were all dressed in black and had teeth like a bat's.

"Won't you sit down and partake of a bite?"

Well, I'm not that daft and said "Not on your life."

I walked out rather quickly and couldn't help feel

They played their parts like they were vampires for real.

Lord Ken told me of battles from previous years.

And showed me cannons and swords, shields and some spears.

When we got to the exit, I said "Thanks for the tour."

But he'd disappeared and wasn't there anymore.

I said to a lady, "I was very impressed,"

"With Ken, werewolves and vampires and how they were dressed."

"We've witches and wizards and zombie-dressed men,"

"But no vampires or werewolves and certainly no Ken."

"This is the only Ken that I know."

"It's only a painting, he died long ago."

"His name was Lord Kenneth McDay," she replied.

"And he's buried in the crypt, that's just outside."

She showed me the portrait and I had to look twice.

I've never been so scared in my life.

I was chilled to the bone and couldn't help feel

That vampires and werewolves really were real.

The face on the wall was that of my host,

And Lord Kenneth McDay was a spine-tingling ghost!!

Nanny Poppin's Pockets

If you need something, my nan's always got it,
In either her bag or one of her pockets.
I don't think she's psychic or that organised,
But it's amazing to see just what is inside.

If you need a pen, there's four to be had.
And paper? Of course there's a miniature pad.
She always has tissues for wiping my nose.
She forgets that I'm no longer three, I suppose.

Nanny always knew when I wasn't well.

A kiss on my forehead and she'd always tell.

And don't worry if you have a nasty fall.

There's cream and a plaster, she's got it all.

Matches for cakes, tablets for aches.

Sugars for tea, biscuits for me.

Three safety pins, a long piece of string.

Needle and thread, white, yellow and red.

But the amount of time, you wouldn't believe,

Nanny can't find her glasses and keys.

'Cos there's the things that go out but also go in.

Her bag and her pockets are used like a bin.

Sweet wrappers and rubbish and umpteen receipts.

Things from our days out, that she'd always keep.

A day at the beach it's seashells and stones

And a trip to the park there are leaves and
pinecones.

There's a song for everything and she makes up the
words.

And has all these sayings that I've never heard.

Like even Stevens and middle for diddle.

Sick as a parrot and fit as a fiddle.

Sometimes I sleep over. I like that a lot.

There's a midnight feast at eight o'clock.

Chocolate and things that I'm not allowed.

And TV in bed. Good job dad's not around.

We're so pleased that Nanny Poppins is ours.

And we can thank our lucky stars,

For a pocket of care and words of love

And a bag full of kindness, squeezes and hugs.

I feel so blessed for all she has done.

For the moments of love and moments of fun.

And why Nanny Poppins? I hear you say,

'Cos she's practically perfect in every way.

The Flea that Fleed

I'm told I look a lot like my mother

And my two hundred sisters and four hundred brothers.

My first home was crowded, we lived on a mouse.

So decided to upsize and look for a house.

I hopped on a cat as one strolled by.

I was very relieved, I'm not going to lie.

In the warmth of a house I was snug as a bug.

Then I dropped to the floor to my home in the rug.

That was all well and good but I needed to eat.

So I looked for the owner and jumped on her feet.

I got off quick when she started to scratch

And after an hour she'd come up in a rash.

She started to hoover to send me away.

When that didn't work she brought out some spray.

I think that's disgraceful in this day and age.

Anyone would think we carried the plague.

My friends and I were very upset.
"I wonder what's bugging her?" I said.
So we decided to go up and jump on her bed.
"That'll teach her to hurt us," another flea said.

She tried tossing and turning and changing the sheet.
She really is selfish. How can I get to sleep?
I decided to hop it. She'd ticked off us all.
So I made my way down and stood in the hall.
I thought it best I should start from scratch.
She'd be even worse when eggs started to hatch.

Along came the postman so I jumped on his trousers.

I figured I'd have the best view of the houses.

I chose a nice cottage on one of the streets.

There was someone inside I was itching to meet.

A cat sat in the window and I sure had a hunch

I'd be moved in and settled in time for my lunch.

Hamish & The Lulu

I'm Hamish the dog. I live in Scotland with Ben.

Sharing his bed, taking walks in the glen.

I worked as a gundog, till I broke a limb.

And Ben rescued me and I rescued him.

I've a straggly coat and I'm slightly deaf,

With one dodgy eye and one gammy leg.

But as Ben was told, when he chose me in Perth,

"Hamish is loyal and friendly and his tail still works."

We were living the life, laid back and carefree.

Late nights on the couch and pizza for tea.

It was just me and him, till one day he wed.

"Meet Susan and her little dog, Lulu," he said.

From that day on, things were never the same.

It was that tiny, fluff ball, the Lulu, I blame.

"Isn't she gorgeous?" everyone said.

No tickles for me, she got them instead.

A Lulu, I found, was a pedigree breed,

Who got all the fuss and the pampering they need.

She goes to a grooming parlour, you know.

I swear once she came back in a dress and a bow.

And they don't eat dog food and biscuits like me.

Oh no, she has chicken or tuna for tea.

The Lulu's so perfect from her head to her paws.

As if I could compete with my many flaws.

She picks up my toys and lays them at my feet.

Even gets in my basket. I mean, what a cheek.

But it was down to that Susan, things came to a head.

She told Ben, I was no longer allowed on the bed.

That was the place where I'd had my best dreams.

Now Lulu sat there, like the cat with the cream.

So next morning, when they were all fast asleep,

I snuck out of the window and ran down the street.

I left the village and stopped by the bench on the hill.

It was where me and Ben would rest and just chill.

Then I walked by the mill and the juniper trees.

Ooh, my favourite place for having a pee.

I saw bluebells and remembered when Lulu had come.

And the smell of the heather, as we'd gone for a run.

How I'd got dripping wet by the reeds in that brook.

And the Lulu got scared by the caw of the rooks.

Was I right in thinking, we'd walked round this loch?

Me, Ben, Susan and Lulu. I'd somehow forgot.

I'd been gone a few hours, I bet they were pleased.

Why would they want an old dog like me?

Scattered sheep on some rocks came into view.

A black and white sheepdog said "Hi. Who are you?"

"I'm Hamish," and told him the chain of events,

Of how nobody loved me and that's why I left.

Sheepdog listened intently and then shook his head.

"Son, you didn't recognise what you had," he said.

"When Lulu got in your basket, did you not realise,"

"She wanted your company and to share some of your time?"

"She picked up your toys and brought them to you,"

"Hoping to play with a ball or a shoe."

"If I had a sister, I'd like to hope,"

"I'd love and protect her and show her the ropes."

113

"As for the bed, was she thinking of you?"

"Could it have been, there just wasn't room?"

"Or maybe, so you both slept with each other,"

"And bonded as baby sister and brother."

"You said Ben chose you, from all of those dogs,"

"He's loved you for years, how much more do you want?"

"Okay, you're scruffy, not the best looking by far."

"But have you ever thought, that's part of your charm?"

I knew he was right and I had been wrong.

I'd made them think that they didn't belong.

I'd had a great family, but I couldn't see,

That I should have loved them, as they had loved me.

I thanked the wise sheepdog for telling me that.

But I was totally lost. How would I get back?

I thought of the places I'd been in the past.

If I retraced my steps, I might have a chance.

Passed the sheep on the rocks and the path round the loch.

The reeds by the brook and the caw of the rooks.

The bluebells in the wood, where the heather smelt good.

To the juniper tree, where I'd had a pee.

Right round the mill, till I got to the hill.

It was raining when I had got back to the bench

And got underneath as I'd lost all my strength.

I dreamt I heard someone calling my name.

"Hamish," over and over again.

I opened my eyes to a wonderful sight,

The Lulu was there and someone shone a light.

Ben carried me gently back to the car.

I could tell by his face, he had taken it hard.

"Hamish," he said, "Never leave me again."

"What would I have done, if I'd lost my best friend?"

Even Susan was crying and sighed with relief.

Made me promise with kisses, that I'd never leave.

At home, the Lulu and me were wrapped up in a rug.

We all sat on the bed and had tickles and hugs.

No longer just pets, but a real family.

My mother, my father, my sister and me.

The First Fall Of Snow

"Look out of the window. It's been snowing all night."

Isla pulled back the curtain and shrieked with delight.

Her garden and slide were white as could be.

"Can I go out there? Mummy please let me."

"First put on your coat and mind how you go."

"I'll be the first one to leave prints in the snow."

She got all wrapped up and stepped out the door.

Isla couldn't believe it, someone had been there before.

"Are those footprints yours?" she asked the cat.

"No they are not. Mine are more dainty than that."

"Have you spoilt my fun?" she said to a mouse.

"Definitely not mine," she said with a flounce.

To a bird on the barrow, "Then they must be yours."

"Nothing like mine, you can be assured."

"Why don't you follow and see where they go?"

"It's really quite easy in this very white snow."

119

"But wait," said the cat. "You should think this thing through."

"It may be a fearsome fox waiting for you."

"Or an enormous eagle," said the mouse with a squeal.

"With a very sharp beak and talons of steel."

"Or a ravenous rat," said the bird on the barrow.

Who they all knew was terribly afraid of her shadow.

Isla stopped in her tracks and gave it some thought.

"I need to find out and I need your support."

So they followed the footprints all in a line.

Isla in front, her friends right behind.

They were led to a flowerpot turned on its side.

And heard a low rumble that came from inside.

But it wasn't a rat, or a fox, or an eagle,

But a cute little puppy that looked like a beagle.

"You poor little doggy. Why are you here?"

"Get in my coat. You've got nothing to fear."

"I would say I'm lost and a long way from home,"

"But I don't think I've got one. I'm all on my own."

"Not from now on," said the bird, cat and mouse.

"Isla will let you live in her house."

Mummy and Daddy put a rug in a box,

"We'll get him a collar when we go to the shops."

"I'm going to call him Frosty, I think,"

"Cos he came with the snow." And he gave her a lick.

Frosty melted their hearts, like the sun melts the snow.

The ice disappeared but their love was to grow.

Mermaids & Miracles

When I was five, at Sandy Cove Bay,

I met mermaids and pirates on that first holiday.

I think I was six, when I played with a witch.

We'd fly to the moon on a stick for a broom.

And in my garden, where the long grass grew

Was where pixies lived and fairies flew.

I made them houses and acorn beds

And we'd hide from the trolls in the garden shed.

A pink unicorn would come for tea

And a prince once asked to marry me.

As the marks of my height, on the wall got high,

Child-like things had passed me by.

The more I grew, the less I saw.

Maybe I didn't believe anymore.

But when we went back to Sandy Cove Bay,

My son saw a mermaid, I heard him say.

He dug in the sand for an old treasure chest

By reading a map that the pirates had left.

Then to our house, a wizard came.

Inventing spells was their favourite game.

With monsters to fight when he played with his friends

From under the stairs where they'd made their den.

Years later, my grandson stayed for the night.

There were ships to sail and pirates to fight.

And in the garden, by my old shed,

The fairies had gone, there were dragons instead.

But now that I'm old, I don't feel sad.

I remember the magical times I had.

And I didn't think I'd see any more

Of the mystical creatures like I had before.

Then just like that, I could suddenly see

A sparkling angel in front of me.

She said "Come with me," and took my hand.

"I'll take you home to a wonderland."

"Where rainbows never need the rain,"

"And you'll see all those things that you loved, once again."

The Witch of Ridgebone Manor

Chapter 1

Beside the Seaside

"Who can see the sea?" said Emma.

"Me," said Oliver and Lucy in unison. George and James were too busy on their phones to answer, but even they looked up to see the roads and fields give way to the blue on the horizon.

Darren was driving and his wife, Emma, was excitedly pointing out the sights of Brighton to the five children sitting in the back. His youngest daughter, Rose, was fast asleep in her car seat.

"Are we nearly at Auntie Lou's yet?" asked a very bored George. "It's taking ages."

"Five more minutes. And before we get there, I want you all to be on best behaviour for Auntie Louise and Uncle Alex when we've gone. Don't break anything and you boys look after your little sisters. We'll be back on Monday, so you've got a whole weekend. I wish it was warmer, but at least it isn't raining. Here we are, Arundel Terrace. It's that house there."

"Wow," said Oliver. "It's huge."

"Wait till you see inside," said Darren. "Theirs is on the second floor, so you've got a lovely sea view." Two huge white pillars stood either side of the large porch of the regency house.

Emma pressed the button for number six, but Louise was already opening the big, black door to greet them.

"Hello. Come in, come in. I'll carry little Rose. Oh, she's so cute."

"She slept all the way here. Unlike the others," said Emma, with a big sigh.

"Come on, kids. I'll show you where you are sleeping and then we'll go to the beach."

Alex and Darren carried all the bags and equipment up the two flights of stairs. "How long are they staying again?" asked Alex.

Darren smiled. "I know, but most of it is for Rose, her travel cot and all that. I've got this work's do and the kids will love it here. Hopefully, they'll be no trouble. George is fifteen and James is ten, so they can look after the little ones."

"Well, there's plenty for them to do in Brighton. The pier, Sea Life and I'm sure Louise will want to take them shopping," said Alex. "They'll be fine. Just a normal weekend by the seaside."

Actually, it was anything but normal!!

Chapter 2

The Bird Lady of Brighton

"**C**an we go to the beach now, pleeease, Auntie Lou?" begged Oliver.

"I've just got to give Rose her bottle. I won't be long."

James looked up from his phone. "Me and George can take Oliver and Lucy. You'll be able to see us from the window."

"Okay, but stay together. And don't go near the water and put your coats on, it's chilly out there. Alex and I will join you soon. Take these cakes and drinks for later. You'll need this key to get through the secret garden that only these houses can use. There's a tunnel that runs right down to the beach."

"Cool," said James. "A secret garden and tunnel."

It was nearly the end of October and although the sun was shining, there was a bitter wind blowing in from the sea. When the four children were wrapped up in their outdoor clothes, George, James, Oliver and Lucy went through the private garden and down the long tunnel to the beach.

"Oh," said Oliver, disappointedly. "It's stones, not sand."

"I love pebbles," said Lucy. "I like looking at the shapes and different colours. I'm going to find some with holes in, so I can make a necklace for Mummy."

"And you can skim them on the water," said George. "Come on James."

When the novelty of throwing stones in the water had worn off, George and James walked back to where Lucy and Oliver were collecting pebbles. The sound of screeching seagulls brought the sight of a woman to their attention. She had long, black, straight hair that was long enough for her to sit on and she was wearing an ankle-length, brown skirt with an old green anorak. There were two black bags by her feet. She was throwing broken biscuits up in the air and watching as the quickest gulls caught the pieces, while the slower ones waited by her feet to pick up the fallen crumbs.

Two boys, that George thought looked about seventeen, were coming towards her from the direction of the pier.

"Well, if it isn't the bird lady of Brighton, or Loopy Lil, as I call her," laughed the taller of the boys. "Don't give all your food away, that could be your dinner tonight. There's a bit of old newspaper there, you might need that for a blanket. Go and find yourself a bench and get off our beach." The other boy just sneered and laughed. They hadn't noticed the children until George said "You get off the beach. She's not hurting you." He clenched his fists by his sides.

James stood next to him, giving his fiercest look to the two thugs.

"Oh yes. And who do you think you're talking to?" asked the younger one.

"To you. Leave her alone. Stop picking on her," said James.

"Stop being horrible," added little Oliver.

"Very brave, aren't you all? You won't be so brave when we throw you head first in the sea, will you?"

The lady turned to look at her heroes for the first time and George thought she looked older than he first thought. Heavy lines criss-crossed her face and when she frowned, George thought he heard her say "Tarulla macoola."

Suddenly, the seagulls stopped screeching and flew as one towards the bullies. James said afterwards, it was as if their hair was made of bread, the way they were pecking at them. Flaying their arms didn't stop the attack of the birds and they only managed to get rid of them when they got to the pier.

The children looked at each other in shock. "What happened?" asked James.

The bird lady stared after them. "Ah the birds were just playing with them. They wouldn't hurt anybody. Birds are kind, it's some people that hurt people. But not you children. You stuck up for me and I won't forget that." Her face looked a lot younger, now she was smiling.

"Do you want to sit with us?" asked Lucy. "Auntie Lou and Alex will be here soon. You can have my cake."

"Well thank you. You are very kind. I haven't seen you before. Are you on holiday?" asked the lady, as she sat next to the little girl.

"We're staying with our aunt and uncle for a few days. We've got a little sister with us as well, called Rose. She's a baby, only nine months old."

"Well, your parents must be very proud of you all. But I must go now, but I will remember what you did today. Some look at me and see what they want to see, but you saw beyond that. I see you like stones, like me, Lucy. Here take this one. It's old and dirty but save it for Mummy. It will bring you both good luck."

"Thank you, err lady."

"Isadora. My name is Isadora."

"I'll put it in my jeans' pocket so I don't lose it."

"I'll be off now then. Your aunt will be here any second. And George, I meant it when I said I won't forget. Goodbye, children."

George looked around and was amazed that the bird lady was already out of sight. "Not only that," he thought. "She called her Lucy and knew my name as well."

Chapter 3

The Invitation

Oliver was sitting in the window seat looking out to sea, so he was the first one to see the large car pull up and stop outside the flat. A chauffeur, in a black uniform and peaked cap, stepped into the porch and pressed the buzzer. Louise came to the window and looked down. She recognised the car as a silver, vintage, Rolls Royce.

"Look at that car, Alex. They must have the wrong flat." Louise picked up the intercom phone.

"Can I help you?" she asked.

"I'm here with Lady Isadora Ridgebone. She met the children yesterday and wanted to ask them something as a way of thanks."

"Really? They did tell us about a lady feeding the birds. But they thought she was a …umm. Sorry. Tell her to come up."

They all stared as a tall, beautiful, well dressed woman got out of the car and entered the building.

"Come in, Lady Ridgebone. Nice to meet you. I'm Louise and this is my husband, Alex. I believe you know my niece and nephews."

"Indeed I do. They came to my rescue yesterday."

"So they said. I was very proud of them. Would you like a cup of tea?"

"Thank you, yes." Alex went off to make it. "How long have you lived here?"

"About eight months. We love Brighton. Do you live nearby?"

"Along the coast - Ridgebone Manor. Have you heard of it?"

"Is it that lovely, big house on the hill, overlooking the sea?" asked Louise.

"That's the one. It's been in my family for generations. But this is a lovely area as well. I used to have friends that lived here, in Sussex Square, so I spent many happy hours in the private garden. There were lovely plants and little paths to follow, with hidden seats and statues. Then there's that tunnel to the sea that Lewis Carroll wrote about in Alice in Wonderland."

"I did hear that. His sister lived here."

"That's right, Henrietta. I knew them both. I mean I know of them well," and changed the subject quickly. "Did you know Queen Victoria and Prince Albert used to enjoy a walk round your private garden?"

"No, I had no idea. How fascinating."

They chatted and drank their tea and then she told Louise and Alex why she had called on them.

"My halloween party is quite a big occasion in the town and I would like to invite the children to come as my guests. It's tomorrow night, if you have no objections."

"Well, I don't know…"

"They will be quite safe, I assure you. The Chief Constable of Sussex will be there. Gregory can pick them up at seven thirty and will bring them back at the end. It's the least I can do after what they did for me yesterday."

The children started jumping up and down with excitement. "Looks like they would love to come, Lady Ridgebone."

"Please call me Isadora. Oh yes, I nearly forgot, the party is fancy dress." She stood up. "So it's all sorted, I'll see the four of you tomorrow night."

It took a bit of running around and ingenuity, but by the time the car returned the next day, George was a zombie, James was a vampire, Oliver looked just like Spiderman and Lucy had become her favourite princess, Elsa. Louise had done her blonde hair into a long plait, just like the character in the movie.

At seven thirty exactly, Louise and Alex watched them driving off. They had looked into Lady Isadora and found out she was an eccentric but benevolent millionaire. Once a week she came into Brighton to feed the birds and to bring bags of things for the charity shops. Harmless and slightly potty seemed to be the description of her from most people. George had his phone, so they weren't worried. What could possibly happen?

Chapter 4

Halloween Party

As they entered the large gates and drove up the long drive, a bolt of lightning flashed in the sky, over the large house, like something from an old horror film. Together with the bats that were flying around, George wondered if it was part of a special effect to set the scene for the party. On either side of the drive were laurel bushes, on which were hanging old-fashioned lanterns.

"Trick or treat," said Oliver, when the heavy, creaking door was opened.

"Enter children. My name is Vera. I'm her ladyship's maid. But I wouldn't say trick or treat here, if I were you."

"Why not? I thought you had to on Halloween," said Lucy.

"Not with this lot. You're more likely to get a trick yourself. I said it once and was turned into a squirrel." Then she burst out laughing. "Lady Isadora, here are your special guests."

"Welcome. My, you all look fabulous. George, there's a lot of other zombies here that I can introduce you to. And James, you must be Dracula. I knew your great great grandfather. Hello again, Spiderman. And Lucy, you look the spitting image of Elsa. Do you like my costume, Alice in Wonderland?"

"I thought you might come as a witch, 'cos of your hair and everything?"

"Oh no, George. I wanted to come in fancy dress as well."

George and James gave a puzzled look to each other.

"Now if you want to meet some witches let me introduce you to Elizabeth and Suzanna Pendle. They refused to dress up." George thought they had, as they were the best witch's outfits he'd ever seen. The two sisters were in long, black dresses, woollen shawls and black bonnets. They held out long, bony fingers and shook all their hands.

"Don't worry, kiddlywinks, we haven't eaten any children for centuries. We're not allowed to do jiggery pokery like we used to."

"Your witch make-up is very good," said Oliver.

"I haven't worn any for years. When you're as beautiful as us, you don't need make-up," said Suzanna and they both cackled.

"Shouldn't your hats be pointed though?"

"I don't know who started that idea. I've never seen a witch in a pointed hat in all my years."

"And that's a lot of years, four hundred," laughed her sister.

"Are we going to play games, like bobbing for apples?" asked James.

That stopped the sisters laughing. Elizabeth Pendle put her hand on her chest. "Don't even think of that, boy. Whatever next. Come, sister, let's go and have something to eat. I saw a delicious beetle and mushroom quiche over there."

"They really get into the spirit of it, don't they, Isadora?"

"Spirit. Ah, very funny, George. Very clever. Do get yourselves a drink."

Oliver looked around. "I love all the decorations." There were skeletons and various heads fixed to the walls. In the centre of the ceiling was a huge chandelier, made up of bones and skulls, instead of crystals. "Where did you get them? My mum would love them."

"Oh, Gregory digs them up every year... I should say digs them out," said Isadora, with a smile. "And now I must leave you, Queen Cleopatra has just arrived."

"Is it me, James, or is something strange going on here?" said George.

"Well, I don't think it's you. The costumes look a little too real for my liking. That vampire that's talking to Cleopatra looks like he's going to have a drink any minute and I don't mean out of a glass. Come on, let's have a look around. Lucy, you stay here and play with those twins over there. The ones that ...err...don't look scary at all."

The three boys crept up the grand staircase and on to the landing, from where they could see all the guests. As they expected, there were witches and warlocks and many famous figures from history. In the corner, a lady in a medieval costume was playing a harpsichord and an old man was playing the violin. There was talking and laughing and the boys began to think they were imagining things, as some of the guests looked like they were gliding over the floor, rather than walking.

They heard the sound of voices and footsteps coming towards them, but couldn't see anyone, so they ran to the corridor on their left and started laughing.

"That was scary," said Oliver. James and George looked behind them and saw a man, dressed as a monk, walk away from them and disappear through the wall. George rubbed his eyes and looked again. They walked to where the man had been, but the only thing there was a full-length mirror in an ornate silver frame.

"Is it a door?" asked James.

"No, it doesn't open. It must be though. Otherwise...."

"Otherwise, that means he must be a..."

Suddenly they all jumped out of their skins. "Must be a what?" said Isadora, loudly.

George spoke first. "We were wondering if this house is haunted? Because we thought we saw a man or a ghost, just disappear straight through this wall."

144

"Of course it's haunted. But he wasn't a ghost…"

"Thank goodness for that."

"No, he was going back to his own time, long, long ago in the past."

"Wow, so he was travelling back in time?" asked James. "So, all these people are from another time?"

"Oh no," said their host. "Most of them are ghosts!"

Chapter 5

The Ghosts of Ridgebone Manor

Isadora put her arm around James to lead the boys back to look over the bannister. "They come on Halloween every year. I'm quite famous for my parties. The Queen even came once."

"You've met Queen Elizabeth?"

"No, dear, Queen Victoria."

"So," George said, "Some people are from different times and not ghosts?"

"Vera, my maid, is a ghost. As is Florence Kindheart over there. You must meet her. She was on the Titanic. Don't worry, Oliver, we are all friendly here. See Mary and Ruth over there, dressed in white? They're absolute angels."

"You mean they're really nice?"

"No. I mean they are real angels."

"Uh-oh. So does that mean that man over there with the horns and the red cape is ......?

"Yes, Oliver, I'm afraid so…. That is Mr Barton who owns the bakers in town," and she burst out laughing. "Many here are just humans, like yourselves. And everyone else wouldn't hurt a fly. The only one you have to watch out for is my old enemy, Jason Darndell. He's an evil witch and wizard catcher from four hundred years ago. He wants to rid the world of all witchery, whether they are good or bad, especially me. He never gives up. Jason shouldn't be here, but he may have slipped in without me noticing." She gave a shiver. "He may be close. I can feel it in my bones. And a Ridgebone's bones are never wrong. Last time I had to use a spell that turned him into a magpie. That's why people started saying to see one magpie was unlucky, because of Jason Darndell in 1780. But these spells can wear off after time. So do look out for him. He wears a tall, green hat and his white hair is tied back in a ponytail."

"You mean like that man who's talking to my little sister?" said a horrified George, pointing towards the very man!!

Chapter 6

Jason Darndell Returns

"So let me get this straight, girl. You're Elsa and when you take off your gloves, with just your bare hands, you can turn all around you into ice?" said the despicable Jason.

"Yes, I told you. If I get angry I turn everything into ice and it's winter forever," said Lucy. The evil man started rubbing his hands.

"So you have the power over water. Have you always had the gift?"

"I suppose so. I nearly killed my sister, Anna, when we were young, when we were making a snowman."

"You can even turn a man into snow?" Jason couldn't believe his luck. He'd only been at the party for a few minutes and had already found the most powerful witch he'd ever met. "Can you turn me into a snowman?"

"Don't be silly. I only do things like that when I am angry. Although you are beginning to make me a bit angry with all these stupid questions. Do you like my ball gown?" asked Lucy. "My auntie got it for me."

"Does she have the gift as well?"

"Well, she gets a lot of gifts from Uncle Alex, so yes."

The witch catcher was getting very excited now. "So, you have a sister, an auntie with the gift and an uncle with the power."

"Well, I'd say Auntie Lou tells Alex what to do more actually…"

"Jason, I don't remember giving you an invitation," shouted Isadora, making the weaselly man jump a foot in the air. George put a protective arm around his sister.

"Good evening, Isadora. This time I am not after you. I have found someone who could turn us all into ice and make all seasons to be winter forever, just with the sweep of her hand. And she admits it!"

"She wouldn't be called Elsa, by any chance, would she? Stupid man. Oh Jason, you do make me angry picking on a little girl." George looked at her and noticed she looked like she had on the beach, wrinkled and angry looking.

"Periscon Murinas," she growled as she fixed her eyes on Jason and shrunk him before their very eyes into a little mouse. "Don't worry, children, he's a lot less trouble like this. Come on, let's take him back to where he belongs." Her face was once again smooth and young.

They were all too shocked to speak, so they followed Isadora silently up the stairs to the passage with the door to the past and future. "Farewell, Jason Darndell. Back to your own time and don't come back," said their friend, as she put the squeaking mouse, still with his green hat on, through the mirror.

As she did so, a girl stepped through from the other side. "Hello. Am I in the right place for the party?" She was a lovely, young lady of about seventeen with long brown hair and wearing a pink evening dress.

"You are indeed, but I don't remember you, I'm afraid," said Isadora.

"My name is Rose. I'm staying in Brighton with my Aunt Louise and Uncle for two weeks, before I start my new job in London." She looked closely at Lucy. "I seem to know you. You look so familiar. Perhaps you are friends with my brothers, George, Oliver and James."

Before Lucy could answer, Isadora took Rose's arm and led her back through the mirror.

"Sorry, but you are a bit early, my dear. About sixteen years in fact. Things could get very complicated if you stay. There's a time and a place for everything and this is the wrong time for you."

"Was that our baby sister, Rose?" said George. "I think it's about time you tell us exactly who you are, Lady Isadora Ridgebone."

Chapter 7

Rags to Witches

"I'm from a long line of witches. We weren't always rich, but my great great grandfather put a curse on the Spanish Armada for Elizabeth I and was given Ridgebone Manor and was made a Lord. Witches have a bad reputation, but we never hurt anyone - unless they deserve it, of course. We help to heal when we can and cast love spells a lot more often than curses. Once you've saved a witch, they will repay you forever. I'm only thirty of your years but I've been of this world for over five hundred years. The reason I'm dressed as Alice in Wonderland is that I'm the one that showed Lewis Carroll the tunnel from your aunt's garden over a hundred and fifty years ago. And also Charles Dickens got the idea of A Christmas Carol when he came to stay here in, ooh, must have been in 1842."

"I love that story," said Oliver. "I get it, the ghosts of past, present and future."

"Precisely. I never get any credit though. Don't get me started on when that chap found a lion upstairs in my wardrobe. I should be a billionaire by rights. Is there anything else you want to ask me before we go and enjoy the rest of the party?"

"Can you see the future, in tea leaves or read palms?" asked James.

"Of course. I only do it once in a blue moon now. It was doing that many years ago that got me noticed by Jason Darndell. I predicted the fire of London two years before it happened. But it just happens to be a blue moon tonight. Right, let me concentrate."

She put her hand on their foreheads one by one. "James, you've just bought a guitar, keep playing, but you will be a businessman and make a lot of money. George, you will have three children and a very happy life. Oliver, you love drawing and one day you will be making films and live in America. Lucy, you are very clever and will work on computers but your first love is singing and you will dance and sing on the most famous stage in England. Your sister, Rose also will succeed in all she does and find happiness with a man called Matthew.

When you see your mother, tell her that the colour red and the number 22 will bring her what she needs. I used to tell fortunes, but there was no future in it," chuckled Isadora. "Just a little witchy humour there for you. Come on, let's get back to the celebration of the witching hour. The party ends at the stroke of midnight, not a second later. Some of my guests still need to haunt for a living."

They spent the rest of the night listening to a singer called Elvis Presley and watched a magic trick performed by The Great Houdini. But all the wizards guessed how he had done it, so they weren't very impressed. Oliver was enjoying the buffet till he realised he had misheard the word human for hummus, just before he put it on a cracker!! And to be honest, the chicken drumsticks and spare ribs looked a bit suspect to him too. Also the vampires seemed to be enjoying a glass of tomato juice a bit too much, in his eyes.

Lucy danced with a real live Prince, well not live, of course. While James and George learned all about life as a zombie, well not life as such.

All four children had the most exciting night ever, but would anyone believe them?

Chapter 8

A Letter from the Past

"So, Isadora is really a witch and you met Elvis Presley? And there was some sort of doorway to the past and future?" said their mother, Emma, on the Monday afternoon when she came to collect them.

"And we met real angels and ghosts. Don't you believe me?" asked Oliver.

"Of course I do, darling. And a man was turned into a mouse. Sounds highly possible to me, doesn't it to you, Darren?"

"Definitely. I trust you," said Darren, while laughing. "Thousands wouldn't. You could write stories with that imagination." Oliver walked off to find the others. Louise and Alex hadn't believed them either.

Louise walked into the sitting room. "I did their washing, Ems. Here you go. I found this in Lucy's jeans' pocket.

"That's my pebble. Isadora gave it to me on the beach for good luck. It was all dirty and brown, but look, Mum, it's bright red. She said I've got to give it to you one day."

Emma held it up to the light. "Look at that. Ruby red."

Lucy remembered what she had to tell her mum then. "Isadora said to tell you that 22 is your lucky number and red will bring you exactly what you need."

Was Isadora going to be proved right!!

Emma and Darren decided to drop in on Lady Ridgebone on the way home, to thank her for giving their children such a special time. They all hugged and thanked Louise and Alex for their perfect weekend. The drive up to the manor house didn't look so scary in the daytime and none of the children were worried about knocking on the door, even if it was opened by a ghost called Vera. But a plump lady in a black and white uniform opened the door this time.

"I'm terribly sorry, but Lady Isadora is out at the moment, but she asked me to give you this letter and her apologies." She went to shut the door. "Excuse me," asked James. The maid called Vera, where is she?"

"Vera Harper? She died on Halloween years ago. Funny thing is, some people swear they've seen her. But that's impossible as you well know." And this time she did slam the door on them.

"How on earth did she know we were coming?" said Mum. But the children weren't surprised at all. "I'll read it. What strange paper. Looks very old. And it's written with a real ink pen in perfect fancy writing. Here we go."

Dearest George, James, Oliver & Lucy,

So sorry that I missed you today. It was kind of your parents to come and thank me, but it's I who should be thanking them for having such wonderful children. I do hope you enjoyed the party. It's my favourite day of the year, where ghosts, ghouls and goblins can get together in celebration. I didn't get to see baby Rose for long, but her time will come. I feel it in my bones that we will all meet soon. And as you know a Ridgebone's bones are never wrong. You'll be pleased to know the little problem of the mouse seems to be over, for now. Please remind your mother that her lucky number is 22 and the colour red.

Must dash. I'm on my way to Waterloo to see my old friend, the Duke of Wellington. He is in need of my help.

Till next time.

Love and luck

Isadora.

"Has she got mice in this big old house? I'm not surprised," said Emma

"Only one, called Jason," said George.

Oliver groaned "I told you, Mum, Isadora turned a man into a mouse. And you say I never listen."

"You really must stop making up these stories, Oliver. But that's not the only odd thing."

"What's odd?" asked Darren.

"The date at the top. She's written July 18th 1815!"

Chapter 9

A Wickedly Good Witch

November came and went and before long all thoughts were about Christmas. Oliver and Lucy had already written their lists of wanted presents. George and James were dropping hints every time an advert came on the television. Emma wasn't excited. Money was tight that year and although she wanted to get the children everything they wanted, she knew she'd have to cut right back that year. Bills were piling up quicker than the Christmas cards. They needed a miracle. Which was exactly what they got when a red envelope landed on the mat.

"Come here, kids. You've got a Christmas card from Isadora."

"Isadora from Brighton?" asked an excited Oliver.

"Yes. Listen all of you."

My dearest friends, I hope you are having a wonderful time. I shall be in your area for the festivities. Do you think your parents would give me permission to take you all to tea on Christmas Eve? If I don't hear from you, Gregory and I will pick you up at 4 o'clock. Baby Rose will be very welcome to come too. Wrap up warm. You never know where we may go.

Lucy, my dear, now is the time to give your mother that pebble. Remember I said it will be just what she needs. Red is her lucky colour. And that is a ruby red real ruby! Tell her to take it to the jewellers shop in town. She will get five thousand pounds for it. I feel it in my bones. And a Ridgebone's bones are never wrong.

Love and luck

Isadora.

And she was right. Five thousand pounds made all the difference to their Christmas. It was just what Mummy needed. Isadora had known from the first day they met.

Chapter 10

All Aboard

So, by three thirty on Christmas Eve, George, James, Oliver, Lucy and this time, baby Rose, were all dressed in their coats, scarves, hats and gloves waiting to go on their magical outing.

George was the first to see the silver Rolls Royce pull up outside their house. All of the children playing on the nearby swings turned to look at what was happening. The children felt like royalty as the chauffeur opened the door for them. Isadora lowered the window to talk to their mother.

"Merry Christmas, Emma. I'm going to take them on the nearby steam train ride first, if that's alright with you?"

"I know the one. You get mince pies and meet Father Christmas as well."

"Really? The real one?" said a surprised Isadora.

"Err, I suppose so," said an even more surprised Emma.

"Well, I'll know when I see him. Now don't worry, I'll have them safely home by eight o'clock at the latest."

"Thank you again for the wonderful ruby. How can we ever thank you?"

"You already have, my dear. Now have I got Rose's pushchair? Good."

"Are you sure you can manage a baby as well? It's so good of you. It gives me the chance to wrap all the presents."

"I know. Darren's golf clubs will need some clever wrapping so he can't guess what they are."

"However did you know what I got him?"

"Just a lucky guess. And you're going to love Spain. See you later. Gregory, let's get this adventure started."

Emma was left staring after them, wondering how Isadora could possibly know she'd booked Spain for their next summer holiday, all thanks to her lucky ruby.

"Mmmm, lovely mince pies," said James.

"Can we see Father Christmas now?" asked Oliver.

"Coats and gloves back on then."

"He's only in the next room. The queue starts here."

"Yes, but that's not the real one. I checked. We have to get on the five o'clock train. Come on," said Isadora and took them outside. George told her that the timetable said there was one at ten to and at ten past but not one at five o'clock.

"Then what may I ask is that?" she said, as a whistle blew. A big cloud of smoke appeared on the platform and when it had cleared, an old-fashioned carriage became visible. Isadora opened the train door. "All aboard. Gregory, you sit with Rose by the window, she's never been on a train before."

"Where does the train go, Isadora?" asked Lucy.

"It's not just the where, it's the when. We are going to experience a real Victorian Christmas in London, so over one hundred and fifty years ago. And we're going to see my old friend, St Nicholas. You know him better as Father Christmas".

164

Chapter 11

London & Lanterns

The chugging of the train and the rattle of the tracks were eventually silenced when they pulled into the station, which according to the plaque on the wall was called Albany Place. All their mouths opened when they walked through the archway and into a street full of people. There were tiny shops, with little panes of glass and stalls, selling everything from geese to ribbons. There was a choir, dressed in clothes of the time, singing the carol 'Away in a Manger'. The singers were wondering what the baby was sitting in. They'd never seen a pushchair before. And was that girl wearing trousers?

Oliver and Lucy wandered over to look in a toy shop window. A wooden sailing boat and a train set had pride of place. A bearded man in a top hat and a bowtie stood next to them.

"Boy" he said, "What is that on the front of your strange attire?"

"You mean the zip?"

"Yes, where the buttons should go." Oliver undid the zip and did it up again.

"Fascinating. An excellent invention. What's your name, boy?"

"Oliver," he replied.

"Well I never." exclaimed Isadora, as she walked over to them. "It's Charles Dickens, the famous author," she told Oliver and Lucy.

"Hello again, Your Ladyship. Might have known these curiously dressed children were with you."

"Meet Lucy and Oliver. What book are you writing at the moment, Charles?"

"It's about a poor orphan boy who comes to London and meets a gang of pickpockets. Oliver you say? Oliver, yes, I like that. How would you like to be in a book, young Oliver?"

"Yes please, sir."

"It sounds sad but no doubt there will be a twist in the tail?" said Isadora.

"Always, my dear lady. There always has to be a twist... Actually, that's not bad. Oliver Twist. Perfect. I must rush home and start writing. I have great expectations... Ooh, I love that too. Good day Isadora and you two." And with that he rushed off to hail a hansom cab with his cane and sped off.

Isadora took their hands. "Hurry up both of you, it's going to snow any second." As if they were in a snowglobe that someone had shaken, the snow started to fall. Isadora led them down a lane with cobblestones, until they reached a sight that they would never forget.

In front of them was the Houses of Parliament, but what they were so excited about was the River Thames. It was frozen over and as far as the eye could see, there were hundreds of people skating on it. As if by magic, and of course it was, Isadora gave them each a pair of white skates. Now, they'd never skated before, but with those skates they glided across the ice as if they'd been doing it all their lives.

Chapter 12

Time for Tea

When they were too tired to skate anymore, they went to Mrs Plunkett's tea shop, where they had hot chocolate and Victoria sponge cake. There was a small Christmas tree in the corner, decorated with candles, fruit and red ribbon. Holly and ivy was hanging in bunches around the walls. The children were all eating quietly, apart from Rose who was sitting propped up in her chair and was cooing gently. Isadora suddenly started talking.

"Mmm, yes. I couldn't agree more with you. You can say that again, dear."

"Who are you talking to? Not another ghost is it?" said George, looking around, worriedly.

"No, not this time. I'm talking to Rose."

"Babies can't talk."

"Of course they can. It's just about understanding them. And animals of course. Now she is saying how she always has to eat quickly or else you lot won't leave her anything and how she wishes she could have gone skating, but she can't wait to walk... Don't worry, Rose, you take your first steps on January 15th, so not long to wait... She says to tell mummy that she doesn't like any of the orange jars of food. And Lucy, stop taking her pink teddy, that's hers... Really Rose? And she heard you telling Daddy that it was her that knocked over that cup of juice last week, when it was you...."

Lucy frowned. "I think I liked it better when she couldn't talk."

"Well make the most of it. You've got till March 21st. That's when she puts her first sentence together," said Isadora, with a smile. "And now we've got to go and see someone. Who was it now?"

"Father Christmas," said Oliver and Lucy.

George rolled his eyes. "I am fifteen, you know."

"You didn't believe in time travel and ghosts three months ago, so get in the Christmas spirit and let's go and find Santa Claus."

Chapter 13

A Magical Ride

When they left the little tea shop, the snow had stopped and it had become very dark. Gas street lights lit their way as they walked along a narrow road. Gregory flagged down a horse-drawn carriage and said something to the driver. He was an elderly man, with a red cap and red jacket. The carriage was very small and the children thought they wouldn't fit in, but somehow they all got in easily. The driver shook the reins and the grey horses moved forward. Before they reached the end of the road, the horses were galloping and as George and James were facing forward, they were sure they were going to crash into the houses.

But as they shut their eyes in fear, they felt themselves being lifted into the air. When they dared to look, they were sitting in an open sleigh with reindeer instead of the horses and with the real Father Christmas sitting in the front seat. Presents filled the space behind them and they looked over the side and saw London Bridge, St Paul's Cathedral and Buckingham Palace far below them.

Lucy and Oliver didn't stop asking questions all during the ride. Father Christmas also had a long conversation with baby Rose! He asked James and George if they'd been nice all year.

"Not exactly all year," they admitted. But as they were honest they were promised a present. The sleigh started losing height and they saw the station near their home. There weren't any streetlights or houses as they were still in the past. There were only farms and the odd cottage.

They landed safely and Isadora was the first to speak. "Thank you very much for the ride home, Santa. You're an excellent driver. Good luck tonight and promise me you'll bring Mrs Christmas to stay in Brighton with me for Easter, my old friend."

"We'll look forward to it. It's always nice to go somewhere warm for a holiday. Goodbye to all of you and don't forget my milk and a mince pie tonight. Merry Christmas and sleep tight."

"Bye. Thank you for the ride," they all shouted. They got in the Rolls Royce and Gregory started the engine. When he turned the headlights on, all the other cars and houses appeared. Isadora was as good as her word and got them home at 7.59.

"Will we see you again?" they all wanted to know.

"Brighton is lovely in the summer, we didn't get the chance to take my boat out last time. I hope you like pirates and mermaids," she said with a wink. And I hear Jason Darndell has come back through the mirror so I may need your help again. Merry Christmas to you all."

They waved her off with tears in their eyes, hoping the time would go quickly till they could visit her.

Chapter 14

Home Again

Mum and Dad opened the door and they walked into their warm, welcoming sitting room, which was covered in festive decorations. Even after all that had happened on that Christmas Eve, they knew there was nothing like getting home again. Mummy was so happy they were all back together. Before she closed the front door, she noticed the number on it - 22. That was what Isadora meant. That was why 22 was her lucky number. Their home, where whatever the children said, was where the magic happened for her, she was the luckiest lady in the world.

She joined the others as they began to all talk at once of where they had been, but it sounded so unbelievable they gave up. Instead, they cuddled up together and listened to Dad reading 'The Night Before Christmas'. Mum sorted out the mince pie and milk for Santa and some carrots for the reindeer. By ten o'clock they were all tucked up in bed, reliving the magical journey in their dreams.

On Christmas morning five special presents were under the tree from Father Christmas. Of course, they were exactly what they wanted. Outside the snow started falling and children through all the centuries and generations opened their presents and enjoyed the comfort and joy of their family's love.

THE END... for now

About the Author

Ann Parker is a children's author and poet who lives in Hertfordshire. Her first published book was 'Wishing Well World'. She wrote about fantasy worlds in her head to get through an unhappy childhood and has now published a new book of wonderful short stories - 'Magic & Memories', as well as finishing her autobiography 'Next Spring Never Came'.

Ann has recently signed with Canadian singer/record producer, Jim Fidler, to put her stories and poems to music.